# Embraceable Me

## by Victor L. Cahn

A SAMUEL FRENCH ACTING EDITION

## SAMUEL FRENCH

FOUNDED 1830

NEW YORK HOLLYWOOD LONDON TORONTO

SAMUELFRENCH.COM

**ISBN 978-0-573-69898-9**          Printed in U.S.A.          #29705

### MUSIC USE NOTE

Licensees are solely responsible for obtaining formal written permission from copyright owners to use copyrighted music in the performance of this play and are strongly cautioned to do so. If no such permission is obtained by the licensee, then the licensee must use only original music that the licensee owns and controls. Licensees are solely responsible and liable for all music clearances and shall indemnify the copyright owners of the play and their licensing agent, Samuel French, Inc., against any costs, expenses, losses and liabilities arising from the use of music by licensees.

### IMPORTANT BILLING AND CREDIT REQUIREMENTS

All producers of *EMBRACEABLE ME must* give credit to the Author of the Play in all programs distributed in connection with performances of the Play, and in all instances in which the title of the Play appears for the purposes of advertising, publicizing or otherwise exploiting the Play and/or a production. The name of the Author *must* appear on a separate line on which no other name appears, immediately following the title and *must* appear in size of type not less than fifty percent of the size of the title type.

An early version of **EMBRACEABLE ME** was first presented in a staged reading by Theater Voices of Albany in Albany, New York on May 29, 1998. The performance was directed by Eleanor Koblenz. The cast was as follows:

ALLISON ........................................... Sue Caputo
EDWARD .......................................... Victor L. Cahn

**EMBRACEABLE ME** was presented in a developmental production at the 78th Street Theater Lab in New York City on June 14, 2000. The performance was directed by Barry Corlew, with lighting by Alison Brummer, costumes by Nicole Evangelista. The producer/general manager was Rachel Reiner, and the producing consultant was S. Kim Glassman. The production stage manager was Amy Henault. The cast was as follows:

ALLISON ........................................ Dori Thompson
EDWARD ............................................. Sky Vogel

**EMBRACEABLE ME** was presented in a staged reading by Theater Voices of Albany in Albany, NY on October 12, 2007. The performance was directed by Edward Noel Wilson. The cast was as follows:

ALLISON ........................................ Jill Sprotbery
EDWARD .......................................... Victor L. Cahn

The world premiere of **EMBRACEABLE ME** was produced by Rachel Reiner Productions, LLC at the Kirk Theatre in New York City on October 23, 2009. The performance was directed by Eric Parness, with sets by Sarah B. Brown, costumes by Sidney Shannon, lighting by Carolyn Wong, and sound by Nick Moore. The production stage manager was Lyndsey Goode. The cast was as follows:

ALLISON ....................................... Keira Naughton
EDWARD ........................................... Scott Barrow

# CHARACTERS

ALLISON – mid-late thirties, vivacious, assertive
EDWARD – mid-late thirties, reserved, amiable

# SCENE

The Place:  Here.
The Time:  Now.

The play should be performed without intermission.

# SETTING

In a minimal production, the stage may be bare except for a few chairs. A preferable strategy, however, is to divide the playing space into two areas, possibly on different levels. One area should reflect the ordered world of Edward, the other the chaotic existence of Allison. Yet no matter how simple or elaborate the design, two stools should be placed downstage, where the actors may perch when they address the audience for extended periods. Both actors may use both stools, which themselves may be moved to suggest different locales.

Props and technical effects may be employed to the extent that space, budget, and imagination permit.

# COSTUMES

ALLISON wears a stylish skirt or slacks, a blouse, and pumps.
EDWARD wears a casual shirt, trousers, and shoes.

*(**ALLISON** and **EDWARD** enter and walk to the stools.)*

**ALLISON.** *(to the audience)* Did you ever have someone you couldn't forget? You figure things can never work out. Yet no matter where you go or what you do…no matter whom you meet, this person lingers in the back of your mind. Like an old song.

*(She gestures to **EDWARD**.)*

Him. I can't believe it, either, but…

**EDWARD.** *(to the audience)* There's just something about me. I grew up in Manhattan, but after a couple of decades I left. Too many people. Too much noise. Too much –

**ALLISON.** *(to the audience)* Take it from me. It was too many people.

**EDWARD.** *(to the audience)* Now my home is three hours from the city, and my nearest neighbor is a quarter-mile down the road. My place is small, tucked away from passersby. Close to my backyard is a pond, and beyond that are open fields where cows and sheep graze in pastoral tranquility –

**ALLISON.** We get the picture.

**EDWARD.** *(to the audience)* I do have visitors. Some come for professional reasons. Others for personal ones. The point is, they rarely stay. Not long ago, however, a small cyclone struck. She called and said she wanted to see me.

**ALLISON.** *(to the audience)* First time we had spoken in months.

**EDWARD.** *(to the audience)* Seven months. The last words we had exchanged were uttered on the twenty-second. At ten-oh-four. Roughly. This time she told me it was strictly business.

**ALLISON.** *(to the audience)* Maybe I was fooling myself, but…

**EDWARD.** *(to the audience)* She arrived at three-thirty. Early enough so she could drive home that night. Late enough so that if she dilly-dallied…who knows?

**ALLISON.** Let me get this straight. You actually live here? All year?

**EDWARD.** Hm-mm.

**ALLISON.** And you don't miss anything?

**EDWARD.** Only you.

*(to the audience)* Talk about smooth.

**ALLISON.** Don't start.

**EDWARD.** How was the drive?

**ALLISON.** Don't ask.

**EDWARD.** I'm running out of topics.

**ALLISON.** You know how good I am at finding places.

**EDWARD.** No.

**ALLISON.** Yes, you do!

**EDWARD.** Oh.

*(a beat)*

You're so good at finding places! What happened?

**ALLISON.** I don't know! I was on 84, then 44. No trouble at all. Plenty of trees. I suppose if you like that sort of thing…

**EDWARD.** Then that's the sort of thing you'd like.

**ALLISON.** Finally I found that restaurant. What's it called?

**EDWARD.** The Coachman.

**ALLISON.** But I must've taken a wrong turn somewhere, because I ended up on a dirt road surrounded by corn.

**EDWARD.** Ever had it right off the stalk? Scrumptious.

**ALLISON.** I'll take your word for it.

**EDWARD.** *(to the audience)* You can take the girl out of the city, but you can't take the city…you know how it goes.

**ALLISON.** I'll bet those bumps ruined the shocks. Hope they get me back tonight.

**EDWARD.** Perhaps you shouldn't drive at all.

*(a beat)*

You look good. Tired, but good.

**ALLISON.** Up at six this morning. Interview at an art gallery. The owner told me to come at eight, but when I arrived, he wasn't in. I called back, but he couldn't talk to me. I figured, hey, I'm a star. I'll head over. I got there with the sound man and the camera man, but he was gone, so we left. Back at the station, there was a message. Come right over. I grabbed the sound man and the camera man, and drove back. What do you think?

**EDWARD.** He wasn't there.

**ALLISON.** Gone for the day. I told the guys to forget it.

**EDWARD.** Win some, lose some.

**ALLISON.** Can I write that down?

**EDWARD.** I see your show all the time.

**ALLISON.** You really watch?

**EDWARD.** That interview with the ballet dancer? Great stuff.

**ALLISON.** I'm flattered.

**EDWARD.** The interview with the Congressman?

**ALLISON.** Wasn't that something?

**EDWARD.** You blew it.

**ALLISON.** Are you kidding? That was terrific. Everybody said so.

**EDWARD.** You blew it.

**ALLISON.** What do you know about it?

**EDWARD.** I know you blew it.

**ALLISON.** He wouldn't answer my questions! That's why I pressed him!

**EDWARD.** You didn't press him. He played you for a sap.

**ALLISON.** I could go only so far –

**EDWARD.** You blew it. All right?

*(short pause)*

**ALLISON.** Why haven't you called me?

**EDWARD.** Your number's unlisted.

**ALLISON.** I gave it to you.

**EDWARD.** Only the old one.

**ALLISON.** Why didn't you call the station?

**EDWARD.** Why didn't you call me?

**ALLISON.** That's not the question.

**EDWARD.** It is now.

**ALLISON.** You're out here in the boonies.

**EDWARD.** Phone lines reach all the way.

**ALLISON.** Who has time? Some days I feel like I'm chasing my own tail.

**EDWARD.** Is that why you need me?

**ALLISON.** I didn't say I need you.

**EDWARD.** Do you?

**ALLISON.** I could write the thing myself. Without your help.

**EDWARD.** I'm sure you could.

**ALLISON.** I can still write.

**EDWARD.** A lot of people in your job can't.

**ALLISON.** I can.

**EDWARD.** I didn't say you couldn't.

**ALLISON.** You implied it.

**EDWARD.** I was talking about some others.

**ALLISON.** You meant me.

**EDWARD.** I meant the others.

**ALLISON.** I think you meant that I –

**EDWARD.** I said precisely what I meant.

    *(a beat)*

    Happy birthday, by the way.

**ALLISON.** I got your card.

**EDWARD.** I never forget the fourteenth.

**ALLISON.** You could've done something more passionate.

**EDWARD.** I thought about you all day.

**ALLISON.** Don't try to make up.

**EDWARD.** Most of the night, too.

**ALLISON.** Don't start.

(*a beat*)

Someone may phone later. His name's Jerry.

**EDWARD.** He's entitled to call himself anything he wants. Who is he, by the way? Producer? Agent?

**ALLISON.** Fiancé.

**EDWARD.** (*to the audience*) Whoops.

**ALLISON.** Aren't you going to say something?

**EDWARD.** Congratulations. Or is it "good luck"? I never know which to say to the woman.

**ALLISON.** I get "good luck."

**EDWARD.** Then what else is there to say?

**ALLISON.** (*to the audience*) I wanted to see some anguish. That may sound cruel, but I needed to know that he cared.

**EDWARD.** What does Johnny do?

**ALLISON.** Jerry.

**EDWARD.** Sorry.

**ALLISON.** He's in the import-export business.

**EDWARD.** Trouble making up his mind?

**ALLISON.** (*to the audience*) There. As soon as his voice took on that tone, I knew he was jealous.

(*to him*)

He's worldly, sophisticated –

**EDWARD.** (*to the audience*) Unlike guess who?

(*to her*)

And you're passionately in love with him, right?

**ALLISON.** Right.

**EDWARD.** (*to the audience*) Completely unconvincing.

**ALLISON.** In college he was on the heavyweight crew.

**EDWARD.** Now there's a skill that can come in handy. Never can tell when you'll have to row to France. Good-looking, is he?

**ALLISON.** That's the consensus.

**EDWARD.** Hard-working.

**ALLISON.** He's made a small fortune. I expect him to turn it into a large one.

**EDWARD.** Witty? Thoughtful? Devoted to you?

**ALLISON.** Finished?

**EDWARD.** One thing I know. To keep up with you, he has to be special.

**ALLISON.** *(to the audience)* That tone again.

**EDWARD.** *(to the audience)* I think I meant it.

*(to her)*

Are you staying for dinner?

**ALLISON.** Are you inviting me?

**EDWARD.** Do you have time?

**ALLISON.** Are you inviting me?

**EDWARD.** The Coachman has an early-bird special. All the flounder you can eat. More like an early-fish special.

**ALLISON.** Are you inviting me?

**EDWARD.** Haven't I made that clear?

**ALLISON.** The other day on Fifth Avenue I passed this kid. Maybe eighteen. His hand was stuffed in his pocket, and he was holding a paperback book.

**EDWARD.** *(to the audience)* That's how I looked.

**ALLISON.** I remembered the way you used to wander down school corridors. All by yourself.

**EDWARD.** I didn't exactly blend, did I?

**ALLISON.** But you always looked content.

**EDWARD.** And cute?

**ALLISON.** Content.

**EDWARD.** And cute.

**ALLISON.** Okay. Cute.

**EDWARD.** Adorable.

**ALLISON.** Don't push it. Remember the first time we talked?

**EDWARD.** Junior year. October.

**ALLISON.** After Professor Herbert's class.

**EDWARD.** You read that essay out loud.

**ALLISON.** About my uncle's dog.

**EDWARD.** The golden retriever. How is he, by the way?

**ALLISON.** He died.

**EDWARD.** I'm sorry. He was a young man, wasn't he?

**ALLISON.** I meant the dog. My uncle's fine.

**EDWARD.** Glad to hear it. Went by the name of Banjo, right?

*(a beat)*

The dog.

**ALLISON.** *(to the audience)* He never forgets anything about me. Jerry knows the batting average of all the Yankees, but can't remember the color of my eyes. This one? Everything.

**EDWARD.** You were sitting in the dining hall…

**ALLISON.** Next to Eileen and Sharon…

**EDWARD.** Wearing that blue and white outfit. You always looked ready to dance a hornpipe.

**ALLISON.** So you always said.

**EDWARD.** And you were annoyed every time I said it.

**ALLISON.** Then why did you keep saying it?

*(short pause)*

**EDWARD.** I wanted to sit next to you that day.

**ALLISON.** Why didn't you?

**EDWARD.** I wasn't crazy about Eileen or Sharon.

**ALLISON.** They were ready to leave.

**EDWARD.** I didn't know.

**ALLISON.** *(to the audience)* All he did was walk over and speak quietly.

*(EDWARD hesitates, then slowly moves to her.)*

**EDWARD.** That was a beautiful piece you read this morning. I enjoyed it.

*(She looks at him. He scurries away, sits, and reads.)*

ALLISON. *(to the audience)* Then he walked away and ate alone. First time a guy ever complimented me on anything except my looks or my walk.

*(a beat)*

Remember, we were both twenty.

*(She walks to him. To EDWARD)*

Hi.

EDWARD. Hi.

ALLISON. Thanks for the comment about the paper.

EDWARD. You're welcome.

ALLISON. Why don't you join us over there?

*(He peers where she has gestured.)*

EDWARD. I'm happy over here.

*(Pause. His movements suggest that she is standing in his light.)*

ALLISON. Am I in the way?

EDWARD. No.

ALLISON. Would you rather I left?

EDWARD. Not necessarily.

ALLISON. May I sit?

EDWARD. Up to you.

ALLISON. Do you want me to?

EDWARD. Whatever you'd like.

ALLISON. Do you want me…to sit next to you?

EDWARD. We may be making this more complicated than necessary. Why don't you just…?

*(He gestures that she should sit.)*

ALLISON. Thanks very much.

*(She sits.)*

You always seem to have a book in your hand. You must love to read.

EDWARD. Yes.

**ALLISON.** Do I know this one?

*(He holds up the book. She checks the title.)*

Nope. Any good?

**EDWARD.** It shows promise, but I've been disappointed before.

*(pause)*

**ALLISON.** If you want me to leave...

**EDWARD.** I'm sorry. I don't mean to be...It's just that I'm... well, I'm...

**ALLISON.** Extremely articulate.

*(They smile.)*

May I ask a question?

**EDWARD.** You just did.

**ALLISON.** Why'd you like my paper?

**EDWARD.** I thought it was genuine. If someone else had written it, it would've been maudlin. You made it touching. All right?

**ALLISON.** I didn't mean to put you on the spot.

**EDWARD.** Yes, you did.

**ALLISON.** I said I didn't.

**EDWARD.** I know what you said, but that's not what you meant.

**ALLISON.** Stop correcting me. I had enough of that this morning.

**EDWARD.** Herbert was dead wrong. You're a first-rate writer. Why are you so intimidated by him?

**ALLISON.** He's the teacher. I assume he's good at what he does.

**EDWARD.** If he were really good, he wouldn't be a teacher.

**ALLISON.** Anyway, you didn't have to say that.

**EDWARD.** I know.

**ALLISON.** Then why did you?

**EDWARD.** Why?

**ALLISON.** I asked you first.

**EDWARD.** You're not making this easy.

**ALLISON.** I'm not trying to.

**EDWARD.** I've noticed you, too. Especially with your friends.

**ALLISON.** And?

**EDWARD.** You're smarter than they are. You're kinder than they are. And your eyes are absolutely haunting.

*(As he looks at her, she stares back.)*

*(moving away)*

I'm getting more jello. You want anything?

**ALLISON.** No, thanks. I'm going to run a couple of miles.

**EDWARD.** Whatever works.

**ALLISON.** Do you run?

**EDWARD.** There's no place I'm especially eager to get.

**ALLISON.** *(to the audience)* For some reason, I didn't want to leave.

**EDWARD.** *(to the audience)* I didn't want her to leave.

**ALLISON.** *(to the audience)* A couple of days later, I showed him something else I had written.

**EDWARD.** *(to the audience)* A love story. Normally I didn't care for such sentimentality, but she had the right touch.

**ALLISON.** *(to the audience)* He asked me to read it out loud.

**EDWARD.** *(to the audience)* I loved the sound of her voice.

**ALLISON.** *(to the audience)* I kept writing.

**EDWARD.** *(to the audience)* I kept reading.

**ALLISON.** *(to the audience)* Before long, we turned into a team.

**EDWARD.** *(to the audience)* I critiqued her pieces for the newspaper.

*(to her)*

That's the third misplaced modifier. And you have to clean up all those vague pronoun references.

**ALLISON.** Is it worth fixing?

**EDWARD.** Are you kidding? It's great!

**ALLISON.** Well, after you ripped it apart, I figured there was no —

**EDWARD.** Just mechanics! What matters is how you capture this woman! It's incredible. Every day in the cafeteria, she doles out gobs of food to students who ignore her. Then she goes home and barely has enough to feed her own children who love her. You make her so vivid. That's an extraordinary gift.

**ALLISON.** Thank you.

**EDWARD.** Which raises the question of why you write for this rag. Your articles are the only good ones.

**ALLISON.** They can use a topnotch editor.

**EDWARD.** I wouldn't fit in.

**ALLISON.** How do you know I meant you?

*(a beat)*

Where do you fit?

**EDWARD.** With you.

**ALLISON.** I enjoy other people, too.

**EDWARD.** I don't.

**ALLISON.** I can't give up the rest of my friends.

**EDWARD.** Whatever makes you happy.

*(short pause)*

**ALLISON.** Eileen asked about you today.

**EDWARD.** What did she want to know?

**ALLISON.** What the interest is.

**EDWARD.** Between us?

**ALLISON.** Particularly from my side.

**EDWARD.** What did you say?

**ALLISON.** I said I couldn't explain it.

**EDWARD.** Thanks for your support.

**ALLISON.** *(to the audience)* In class I sat in the front. I liked to speak up.

**EDWARD.** *(to the audience)* Even when she didn't know what she was talking about, she always found something to say.

**ALLISON.** *(to the audience)* He sat in the corner.

**EDWARD.** *(to the audience)* Never said a word.

**ALLISON.** *(to the audience)* I played field hockey, and was in the chorus of the fall musical: *Cabaret.*

**EDWARD.** *(to the audience)* I wanted to see her cavorting in that skimpy costume, but…all those people…

**ALLISON.** *(to the audience)* I dated a lot. Parties every weekend. For a while I went out with Todd. He was a fullback.

**EDWARD.** *(to the audience)* He was a lummox.

**ALLISON.** *(to the audience)* Then there was Mike. A swimmer.

**EDWARD.** *(to the audience)* Thick body. Equally thick head.

**ALLISON.** *(to the audience)* I loved to dance. I wanted to dance with him.

**EDWARD.** *(to the audience)* I don't dance.

**ALLISON.** *(to the audience)* But we always talked. Sometimes for hours.

**EDWARD.** *(to the audience)* A lot was light gossip.

*(She sits and lays her legs across his lap. He reacts awkwardly.)*

**ALLISON.** Melissa's a tease, you know. Strings boys along, then dumps 'em. Mark's just the latest. Of course, he's using her, too.

**EDWARD.** Which one is Mark?

**ALLISON.** Tall, big ears –

**EDWARD.** Got 'im. Why do I think he deserves whatever happens?

**ALLISON.** 'Cause of the way he dumped Carly.

**EDWARD.** Right.

*(a beat)*

Who's Carly?

*(to the audience)* But some material was more substantial.

**ALLISON.** Lisa's father ran off with some twenty-year-old chippie. A few months later he came home at three in the morning, pounding on the door.

EDWARD. Did they lock him up?

ALLISON. Not so far, but her mother's hoping.

EDWARD. *(to the audience)* And sometimes the material was strictly personal.

ALLISON. Sometimes I want to conquer the world and make a million dollars! Sometimes I want to run away and hide. Sometimes I want to go out and grab a guy! Just take him home and eat him alive! Sometimes I want someone to hold me in his arms and rock me to sleep. Sometimes I can't wait to jump out of bed and face the day. Sometimes I wake up at night, and it's dark, and I wonder how I can go on for one more moment.

EDWARD. *(to the audience)* I surprised myself when I realized that I understood her.

ALLISON. *(to the audience)* I told him who I liked and who I trusted. And who I didn't.

EDWARD. *(to the audience)* Who was sleeping around. And with whom. And why.

ALLISON. *(to the audience)* Who was taking which drugs. And why. Who was selling which drugs. And where.

EDWARD. *(to the audience)* She dropped it all in my lap. Abuse, addiction, abortion. And those were just the A's.

ALLISON. *(to the audience)* I was never self-conscious in front of him. No matter what I said or did.

EDWARD. *(to the audience)* I helped her over her first major hangover.

ALLISON. *(to the audience)* I wasn't a big drinker, but that night I was too rocky to get back to my place, so I stopped at his. He held my head and splashed cold water on my face. Then I was sick all over his bathroom.

EDWARD. *(to the audience)* Not many people can carry that off. She looked good.

ALLISON. *(to the audience)* He went out with a few other girls, too. Artsy types.

EDWARD. *(to the audience)* Nothing serious. They all chewed gum.

ALLISON. *(to the audience)* One night I asked him if he ever wanted children.

EDWARD. I can't stand them.

ALLISON. Why?

EDWARD. They're short, they're young, and they have no sense of irony.

ALLISON. What were you like when you were young?

*(a beat)*

EDWARD. I was never young.

ALLISON. *(to the audience)* Whenever we were deciding what to do, he'd say the same thing.

EDWARD. What would you prefer?

ALLISON. *(to the audience)* Or if I was upset…

EDWARD. We'll do anything you want. Whatever makes you happy.

ALLISON. *(to the audience)* He also kept my personal life in order.

EDWARD. *(to the audience)* She looked organized, but in some ways she could hardly take care of herself.

ALLISON. *(to the audience)* I was busy.

EDWARD. This bankbook is a mess.

ALLISON. It is?

EDWARD. Yes!

ALLISON. How much am I off?

EDWARD. I don't know. You see, when you make out a check, you're supposed to write down the other person's name. And the amount.

ALLISON. Fix it.

EDWARD. Where's your laundry bill?

ALLISON. I don't know.

EDWARD. And the phone bill?

ALLISON. It's all there.

EDWARD. I don't see it.

**ALLISON.** On the desk. Or the wall.

**EDWARD.** Or the floor?

**ALLISON.** Or the bed.

**EDWARD.** I can't do anything without receipts.

**ALLISON.** Just do it.

**EDWARD.** I'd be glad to, but –

**ALLISON.** Just do it!

**EDWARD.** Why don't you do it yourself?

**ALLISON.** I like when you do it.

(a beat)

So do you.

**EDWARD.** What about the rest of the room?

**ALLISON.** It's perfect.

**EDWARD.** There's food all over the place.

**ALLISON.** Leftovers.

**EDWARD.** This pizza's no good.

**ALLISON.** Sometimes I like it cold in the morning. With tabasco sauce.

**EDWARD.** Not after four days. And look at your clothes. And your shoes. How do you manage to look so terrific?

**ALLISON.** Another gift.

**EDWARD.** (to the audience) Once a week I stopped by to straighten up. Fumigate the refrigerator. Make sure she changed the linen and took the laundry.

**ALLISON.** (to the audience) He never stayed overnight, though. No matter how late it was, he always went back to his room. Which, by the way, was immaculate. If I moved a pencil, alarms went off. One day I told him I wanted to introduce him to the head of the college literary magazine.

**EDWARD.** Wouldn't work out.

**ALLISON.** Why not?

**EDWARD.** Too many people.

**ALLISON.** It's one guy. And he's very quiet.

**EDWARD.** I appreciate the gesture, but –

ALLISON. One guy.

EDWARD. Will you come with me?

ALLISON. *(to the audience)* I took him over. A week later he became an editor.

EDWARD. *(to the audience)* And another world opened for me. Without her, I never would've found it. Still, I was really comfortable only when we were alone.

ALLISON. *(to the audience)* He used to buy me presents. Nothing expensive. Maybe a little pin. Or a picture. No reason, he said.

EDWARD. *(to the audience)* First time I had someone to buy for.

ALLISON. When's your birthday?

EDWARD. Next year.

*(to the audience)* She was the subject of a considerable number of dreams. Sometimes she was in clothes. Sometimes not. Sometimes she was wearing just...well, you get the idea. But I never tried to follow through.

ALLISON. *(to the audience)* I thought about what he'd be like in bed. But our friendship was special. I didn't want to risk it.

EDWARD. *(to the audience)* She was different. What can I say?

ALLISON. *(to the audience)* When my aunt died in a car accident, he was the only one I could talk to. He just put his arm around me and held me close. That was what I needed.

EDWARD. *(to the audience)* That was the first time I saw her cry. I didn't want anything or anyone to hurt her. Even though she kept buzzing around the campus, she seemed so vulnerable. At the same time, I envied her capacity to care so deeply. She felt for everyone. I preferred books to people. Books were usually more stimulating, more congenial, and infinitely more reliable. Besides, if I started a book and didn't like it, I could put it aside. No complications.

ALLISON. *(to the audience)* Sometimes we'd spend an hour or two on the phone.

EDWARD. *(to the audience)* She'd call at six in the morning. Or two at night. I didn't mind.

ALLISON. Hi! You doing anything?

EDWARD. Just sleeping.

ALLISON. Oh, good. Listen, I can't find my registration form.

EDWARD. It's on your desk.

ALLISON. No, it isn't.

EDWARD. Under the biology book.

ALLISON. I already looked there!

EDWARD. Next to the makeup kit.

ALLISON. It's not there!

EDWARD. It has to be there.

ALLISON. I'm telling you. It's lost!

EDWARD. Move your sneakers out of the way –

ALLISON. Wait a minute! I found it.

EDWARD. Yay.

ALLISON. It was in my poetry book.

EDWARD. I should've have known.

ALLISON. I'd say so. Try to be more careful, okay?

EDWARD. I'll do my best.

ALLISON. Do a little better than that. Goodnight!

EDWARD. *(to the audience)* Every call was a kick.

ALLISON. *(to the audience)* Nothing in my life was official unless I discussed it with him.

EDWARD. *(to the audience)* Classes, friends, sports. Men. I even heard the lowdown on "that time of the month." Every detail.

ALLISON. *(to the audience)* If I had to suffer, why shouldn't he?

EDWARD. *(to the audience)* One weekend her parents visited from Connecticut and invited us to dinner. Naturally I didn't want to go, but by the end I was glad I did. She wanted to tell them everything she was doing. Instead they told me everything that Chip, her older brother, was up to. Phi Beta Kappa, championship fencer, attorney. Enough to make anyone sick. She needed to know that they believed in her, and were proud of all she did. They just patted her head and sent her off to play.

**ALLISON.** *(to the audience)* He never discussed his family. But after he met mine, I wouldn't let the subject go.

*(to him)*

When are your parents coming?

**EDWARD.** I don't know.

**ALLISON.** You never talk about them.

**EDWARD.** There's nothing to say.

**ALLISON.** What are they like?

**EDWARD.** Why do you want to know?

**ALLISON.** Because you won't let me meet them.

**EDWARD.** They're in New York.

**ALLISON.** Let's go.

**EDWARD.** Why?

**ALLISON.** I want to meet them.

**EDWARD.** I won't be comfortable.

**ALLISON.** I want to meet them.

*(to the audience)* One Sunday morning we took the train in. During the whole ride, he said barely a word. When we came to their apartment on Third Avenue, I couldn't believe it. His parents never stopped smiling and joking with me. Meanwhile he sat with his face frozen. At first I didn't know what was happening, but gradually I understood. It was all an act. His mother and father talked to me, but not to each other. And they spoke about him as if he weren't in the room. When his father made a joke, his mother didn't laugh. Instead she glared at him as if he didn't have the right to open his mouth. When she commented about anything, his father looked away, as if the sound of her voice pained him. I was sorry I put them all through it. On the ride back, he talked quietly.

**EDWARD.** You know how many kids hope their divorced parents will get back together?

**ALLISON.** Hm-mm.

**EDWARD.** I hope mine split up.

**ALLISON.** Why?

**EDWARD.** Because they'll be happier. Once they probably had something between them. Now it's gone. Each of them still has love to give. Just not to each other.

*(He kisses her gently.)*

**ALLISON.** *(to the audience)* After that kiss, nothing was the same.

**EDWARD.** *(to the audience)* For the first time in a long while, I felt I belonged to someone. I also felt absurdly alone.

**ALLISON.** *(to the audience)* Any time I mentioned another guy, he'd get ironic. Just like today. About my fiancé.

**EDWARD.** Where'd you and Jimmy meet?

**ALLISON.** Jerry.

**EDWARD.** Sorry.

**ALLISON.** At a party. Four months ago.

**EDWARD.** Does he know about all the broken hearts you've left behind?

**ALLISON.** Cut it out.

**EDWARD.** Men strewn helplessly at your feet.

**ALLISON.** You're exaggerating.

**EDWARD.** No, I'm not.

**ALLISON.** *(to the audience)* He's not.

**EDWARD.** Does Joey know we may work together?

**ALLISON.** Jerry!

**EDWARD.** Sorry!

**ALLISON.** I didn't ask.

**EDWARD.** Does he wonder if we ever…?

**ALLISON.** I didn't ask.

**EDWARD.** Why not?

**ALLISON.** Because he didn't ask.

**EDWARD.** Why not?

*(to the audience)* At the end of our junior year, we had to choose where to live for the next term.

**ALLISON.** What about an apartment downtown?

**EDWARD.** Great! I'm taking one myself. You can move close by.

**ALLISON.** I meant one for both of us.

**EDWARD.** Oh.

**ALLISON.** I could bring my dog from home.

**EDWARD.** An animal?

**ALLISON.** You'll love him! We could get a cat, too.

**EDWARD.** Too?

**ALLISON.** How about a parrot? Or a gerbil? How about a guppy?

**EDWARD.** I don't even want a plant.

**ALLISON.** C'mon! Something!

**EDWARD.** I don't like anything growing in my house but me.

**ALLISON.** You'll be crazy about my dog! Hardly ever bites. Just like me.

**EDWARD.** Aren't we too late? All the good spots must be taken.

**ALLISON.** I checked the housing office. There's a place right near Brian, Emily, and Keith.

**EDWARD.** *(to the audience)* Three soccer players.

**ALLISON.** And Karen and Jeremy are going to be down the street. They can drop by all the time.

*(short pause)*

You like them!

**EDWARD.** You really think this would work?

**ALLISON.** Why not?

**EDWARD.** Well, I have my ways, and you have…you know, yours.

**ALLISON.** I'll keep the place neat. Promise.

**EDWARD.** But I have my ways, and…

**ALLISON.** And?

**EDWARD.** And you have yours.

*(pause)*

**ALLISON.** And yours don't include mine.

**EDWARD.** I didn't say that.

**ALLISON.** Then what's your point?

*(short pause)*

Fine. Forget I mentioned it. I'll take care of myself.

**EDWARD.** Don't take it personally.

**ALLISON.** Why would I?

**EDWARD.** Besides, if you go for a single, you have a better chance of getting something really good.

**ALLISON.** How would you know?

**EDWARD.** That's what I've heard.

**ALLISON.** Who talks to you?

**EDWARD.** I'll find a place nearby.

**ALLISON.** Why bother?

**EDWARD.** So we can help each other.

**ALLISON.** I don't need help. Do you need help? I don't.

**EDWARD.** It's good to know someone's there.

**ALLISON.** That'll be ducky!

**EDWARD.** *(to the audience)* She left in a snit. But when we saw each other the next day, she seemed to be over it.

**ALLISON.** I think you're right. We need some space.

**EDWARD.** That's probably best.

*(to the audience)* Two days later she had another plan.

*(to her)*

How's the apartment hunt?

**ALLISON.** It's over.

**EDWARD.** Found something already?

**ALLISON.** I'm spending the semester in England.

**EDWARD.** We didn't talk it over.

**ALLISON.** Do I need your approval?

**EDWARD.** I'd just like to know more about it.

**ALLISON.** One kid dropped out yesterday. And they haven't filled his slot.

**EDWARD.** Me?

**ALLISON.** Only fifteen in the group.

**EDWARD.** I can't go.

**ALLISON.** Tuition's the same –

**EDWARD.** That's not it –

**ALLISON.** You could roam the libraries and bookstores –

**EDWARD.** I can't!

*(short pause)*

Are you doing all this just because I wouldn't take an apartment with you?

**ALLISON.** Are you asking whether I'm going to Europe over a matter of housing?

**EDWARD.** I only meant that –

**ALLISON.** Whether I've scrambled across this campus ten times a day for signatures and references, filled out God knows how many forms, and turned my entire life upside down all because of you?

**EDWARD.** Well, the other day you seemed –

**ALLISON.** What an ego!

**EDWARD.** Fine! We both need a break.

**ALLISON.** Exactly what I was thinking.

*(to the audience)* I left during August. Halfway over the Atlantic, I missed him.

**EDWARD.** *(to the audience)* I moved to that single room off-campus.

**ALLISON.** *(to the audience)* I met people from all over the world.

**EDWARD.** *(to the audience)* I read Dostoyevsky.

**ALLISON.** *(to the audience)* One boy at Oxford had a crush on me. I got drunk in his apartment and threw up. He didn't think I carried it off.

**EDWARD.** *(to the audience)* Then I read Kafka.

**ALLISON.** *(to the audience)* I lost my travelers checks.

**EDWARD.** *(to the audience)* I met a couple of girls from the Literary Society. I still liked to talk about writing, and they like to talk about theirs. In private. Their prose wasn't as good as Allison's. And neither was their company. Even so, the sessions sometimes led to spiritual consolation, which once led to physical consolation.

**ALLISON.** *(to the audience)* The group covered the continent. I didn't do much studying.

**EDWARD.** *(to the audience)* I wanted her. But the next morning I looked over and wondered, why is she still here?

**ALLISON.** *(to the audience)* Twice I thought I fell in love.

**EDWARD.** *(to the audience)* Then I realized that I wanted her to be Allison.

**ALLISON.** *(to the audience)* I was wrong each time.

**EDWARD.** *(to the audience)* I missed her voice. I missed the smell of her perfume on my towels.

**ALLISON.** *(to the audience)* I did have fun. At least, that's what I told myself.

**EDWARD.** *(to the audience)* I missed her using my things. Holding my hand. Laying her head on my shoulder.

**ALLISON.** *(to the audience)* I kept in touch with him by mail. He saved every letter and postcard.

**EDWARD.** *(to the audience)* I still have them. I wonder if she knows.

**ALLISON.** *(to the audience)* He still has them.

**EDWARD.** *(to the audience)* I couldn't wait to see her again.

**ALLISON.** *(to the audience)* I cut the trip short. We met in New York.

*(She sits on his lap, and he puts his arm around her waist.)*

As always, a perfect fit.

*(to him)*

Miss me?

**EDWARD.** Only every hour. How about you?

**ALLISON.** I was with me the whole time, so I was fine. Would you like a vacation together?

**EDWARD.** I've been thinking along those lines.

**ALLISON.** Aren't you getting aggressive?

**EDWARD.** Only with you.

**ALLISON.** A friend of the family works at a resort in the Poconos. She can get us a cabin.

**EDWARD.** How long could we stay?

**ALLISON.** A week. Maybe a little more.

**EDWARD.** Going to be cold.

**ALLISON.** We'll make it warm.

**EDWARD.** *(to the audience)* The next day we left.

**ALLISON.** *(to the audience)* It was a beautiful spot, overlooking a lake.

**EDWARD.** *(to the audience)* The snow was light, so we strolled arm in arm around town.

**ALLISON.** *(to the audience)* We both made dinner. He cleaned up.

**EDWARD.** *(to the audience)* Brisk, sunny days.

**ALLISON.** *(to the audience)* Chilly nights.

**EDWARD.** *(to the audience)* That's when we'd sit by the fire and talk about anything she wanted.

**ALLISON.** *(to the audience)* And that's when things became tense.

**EDWARD.** *(to the audience)* You see, the cabin had two bedrooms.

**ALLISON.** *(to the audience)* When we arrived, we each took one. By reflex, I guess, but...

**EDWARD.** *(to the audience)* We knew what was on our minds.

**ALLISON.** *(to the audience)* We never said it out loud, but...

**EDWARD.** *(to the audience)* We knew.

**ALLISON.** *(to the audience)* The longer we waited, the more intriguing the anticipation became.

**EDWARD.** *(to the audience)* There was also only one bathroom.

**ALLISON.** *(to the audience)* For a couple of days we were discreet. We knocked on the door politely. I'd wait for him. He'd wait for me.

**EDWARD.** *(to the audience)* At strategic moments, we'd air it out.

**ALLISON.** *(to the audience)* But gradually the cabin seemed to shrink.

**EDWARD.** *(to the audience)* We kept bumping into each other.

**ALLISON.** *(to the audience)* Finally, on the third night, I was ready for my bath.

**EDWARD.** *(to the audience)* She always took it the same time. I found some way to occupy myself.

**ALLISON.** *(to the audience)* That night I took it early.

**EDWARD.** *(to the audience)* When she walked out of her room, she was wearing just a towel. I couldn't take my eyes off her.

**ALLISON.** *(to the audience)* He watched intently.

**EDWARD.** *(to the audience)* She loved it.

**ALLISON.** *(to the audience)* I smiled subtly.

**EDWARD.** *(to the audience)* There was nothing subtle about it.

**ALLISON.** *(to the audience)* As I walked into the bathroom, I let the towel drop.

**EDWARD.** *(to the audience)* She didn't close the door. I waited until I heard her splashing around. Then I walked in.

**ALLISON.** *(to the audience)* I didn't bother covering up.

**EDWARD.** *(to the audience)* She just leaned back and smiled.

**ALLISON.** *(to the audience)* He sat on the edge of the tub.

**EDWARD.** *(to the audience)* I rolled up my sleeves, picked up the cloth, and began to wash her shoulders.

**ALLISON.** *(to the audience)* Heaven.

**EDWARD.** *(to the audience)* I was inspired.

**ALLISON.** *(to the audience)* I closed my eyes. He moved all over.

**EDWARD.** *(to the audience)* Her neck and back.

**ALLISON.** *(to the audience)* My arms, then my legs.

**EDWARD.** *(to the audience)* Very, very slowly.

**ALLISON.** *(to the audience)* When I opened my eyes, I felt as if I were coming out of a dream.

**EDWARD.** *(to the audience)* Neither of us said a word.

**ALLISON.** *(to the audience)* I just smiled.

**EDWARD.** *(to the audience)* When I reached for the bath towel, she stepped out of the tub.

**ALLISON.** *(to the audience)* As the water dripped off, I stood and waited for him.

**EDWARD.** *(to the audience)* I took my time.

**ALLISON.** *(to the audience)* The towel was thick and fluffy, and almost as long as I was. He bundled me up inside, then carefully dried me all over. He knew just how to maneuver.

**EDWARD.** *(to the audience)* She seemed to purr.

**ALLISON.** *(to the audience)* Sometimes everything's just right.

**EDWARD.** *(to the audience)* We kissed.

**ALLISON.** *(to the audience)* He led me to the living room.

**EDWARD.** *(to the audience)* I laid her down next to the fire.

**ALLISON.** *(to the audience)* He settled next to me.

**EDWARD.** *(to the audience)* I unwrapped the towel. As if she were a birthday present.

**ALLISON.** *(to the audience)* And on that January night, everything fell into place.

**EDWARD.** *(to the audience)* All night.

**ALLISON.** *(to the audience)* And the next day.

**EDWARD.** *(to the audience)* And the next. We didn't do much more walking.

**ALLISON.** *(to the audience)* Mostly to my bed. Then back to his.

**EDWARD.** *(to the audience)* Then to the bathtub. I don't think either of us will ever forget that week.

**ALLISON.** *(to the audience)* Six days.

**EDWARD.** *(to the audience)* And nights.

**ALLISON.** *(to the audience)* Then we rested. After that, the whole world seemed different.

**EDWARD.** *(to the audience)* Even though we were just heading back to school.

**ALLISON.** *(to the audience)* Our first stop was my new apartment.

**EDWARD.** *(to the audience)* I was thinking of moving in, so we cleaned up.

**ALLISON.** *(to the audience)* He cleaned. I supervised.

**EDWARD.** *(to the audience)* Then we lay on the couch.

**ALLISON.** *(to the audience)* At peace with the world.

**EDWARD.** *(to the audience)* I felt I could stay like that, with her in my arms, for a century.

**ALLISON.** *(to the audience)* Until Brian and Emily showed up.

**EDWARD.** *(to the audience)* She hadn't seen them in months. The excitement was palpable.

**ALLISON.** *(to the audience)* We had so much catching up to do.

**EDWARD.** *(to the audience)* She screamed and jumped up. Right away I felt a familiar knot in my stomach.

**ALLISON.** *(to the audience)* In a little while, a whole bunch of people came to welcome me back.

**EDWARD.** *(to the audience)* It became noisy and crowded and…impossible. Within five minutes, I had to get out.

**ALLISON.** *(to the audience)* I wanted him to stay.

**EDWARD.** *(to the audience)* I couldn't.

**ALLISON.** *(to the audience)* He looked back and smiled, then closed the door.

**EDWARD.** *(to the audience)* And settled into my own place.

**ALLISON.** *(to the audience)* I felt bad, of course. He had such a forlorn expression on his face. And the last thing I wanted to do was hurt him.

**EDWARD.** *(to the audience)* But I understood.

**ALLISON.** *(to the audience)* I needed to be part of the action.

**EDWARD.** *(to the audience)* Besides, the next day I was back visiting.

**ALLISON.** *(to the audience)* And everything returned to normal.

**EDWARD.** *(to the audience)* Before long, though, more serious complications arose.

**ALLISON.** *(to the audience)* With graduation in sight, my life was just beginning. I wanted to meet new people.

**EDWARD.** *(to the audience)* I didn't.

**ALLISON.** *(to the audience)* I wanted to find out about the world.

**EDWARD.** *(to the audience)* I knew as much about the world as I cared to.

**ALLISON.** *(to the audience)* I wanted to try, to see, to go.

**EDWARD.** *(to the audience)* I didn't.

**ALLISON.** *(to the audience)* So how could we...?

**EDWARD.** *(to the audience)* I didn't know, either.

**ALLISON.** *(to the audience)* During the spring I accepted an entry-level spot at a television station in Chicago. I figured it would give me a chance to write, plus keep other options open.

**EDWARD.** *(to the audience)* My plans were less certain, so I stayed in New England and joined that great Legion of the Lost known as graduate school.

**ALLISON.** How are we going to see each other?

**EDWARD.** We won't. At least for a while. Unless you care to give up Chicago.

**ALLISON.** Aren't there schools in Illinois?

**EDWARD.** None of them offered me anything.

**ALLISON.** Did you apply?

**EDWARD.** I don't want to go there.

**ALLISON.** Then why don't you just say so?

**EDWARD.** I did!

**ALLISON.** What are we supposed to do?

**EDWARD.** Go our own way.

**ALLISON.** That's it?

**EDWARD.** You're not giving us any choice.

**ALLISON.** I'm not! What about you?

**EDWARD.** I know where I want to live, and I'm going there.

**ALLISON.** Whether I want to or not.

**EDWARD.** I didn't put it that way.

**ALLISON.** How did you put it?

**EDWARD.** I explained that –

ALLISON. I can't give up my life and follow you to Cow Hampshire!

EDWARD. I'm not asking you to!

ALLISON. I need to do what's best for me.

EDWARD. I never would've guessed!

ALLISON. Are you implying that I'm selfish?

EDWARD. I didn't say that.

ALLISON. Did you mean it?

EDWARD. I didn't say it!

ALLISON. Then what did you mean?

EDWARD. I have to think of myself!

ALLISON. And you're calling *me* "selfish"?

EDWARD. No!

ALLISON. Then what are you saying?

EDWARD. That this is never going to be easy.

ALLISON. *(to the audience)* That was the only thing we could agree on. So after graduation, we went our different ways.

EDWARD. *(to the audience)* But we promised to keep in touch.

ALLISON. *(to the audience)* Over the summer and fall, we exchanged phone calls every other day.

EDWARD. *(to the audience)* I called first.

ALLISON. *(to the audience)* I wanted to know that he missed me, too.

EDWARD. *(to the audience)* We slipped to once a week. Then whenever we thought of it.

ALLISON. *(to the audience)* For several months, we hardly kept up at all.

EDWARD. *(to the audience)* I was tempted to call, but somehow...

ALLISON. *(to the audience)* There were nights when I was aching to hear his voice, but...

EDWARD. *(to the audience)* I finished my master's and weighed going for my doctorate, but the thought of further placating academics didn't appeal, so the next spring I took a job as copy editor in the publications office of a nearby college. Not long after, we had our first face-to-face conversation in two years.

**ALLISON.** *(to the audience)* I had to visit Boston for a shoot.

**EDWARD.** *(to the audience)* I took a deep breath and drove to meet her.

**ALLISON.** *(to the audience)* I was actually nervous. With him!

**EDWARD.** *(to the audience)* We kissed, but…

**ALLISON.** *(to the audience)* It was awkward.

**EDWARD.** *(to the audience)* I didn't know how close to hold her.

**ALLISON.** Did I tell you I met the Mayor?

**EDWARD.** When?

**ALLISON.** He visited the station. He likes me.

**EDWARD.** Why wouldn't he?

**ALLISON.** A guy on his staff said there might be a spot for me.

**EDWARD.** With the Mayor?

**ALLISON.** How about that?

**EDWARD.** Nice fella?

**ALLISON.** The Mayor? I'd say so –

**EDWARD.** The guy on his staff.

**ALLISON.** We hit it off.

**EDWARD.** Figures.

**ALLISON.** What does that mean?

**EDWARD.** Nothing.

**ALLISON.** Why do you care about him?

**EDWARD.** I don't. Do you?

**ALLISON.** What is this?

**EDWARD.** Idle conversation.

**ALLISON.** We've been going out for a couple of months.

**EDWARD.** And?

**ALLISON.** And what?

**EDWARD.** You like him?

**ALLISON.** Yes.

**EDWARD.** How much?

**ALLISON.** Hard to say.

**EDWARD.** How close have you gotten?

**ALLISON.** Close.

**EDWARD.** How close?

**ALLISON.** Why are you grilling me?

**EDWARD.** Let's put it this way. You two visit any cabins?

**ALLISON.** I'm not going to answer that.

**EDWARD.** You just did.

**ALLISON.** No, I didn't!

**EDWARD.** Anything else?

**ALLISON.** You sure you're all right?

**EDWARD.** What else is new?

**ALLISON.** I've started working in front of the camera.

**EDWARD.** Tired of writing?

**ALLISON.** My material's been a little flat. I think I need inspiration. And getting out and meeting people might help.

**EDWARD.** What helps your writing is more writing. What you're doing is avoiding real work.

**ALLISON.** It's a different kind of work! Which the people at the station seem to appreciate. Besides, I have the personality for it. And maybe the ego.

**EDWARD.** No doubt you have both.

**ALLISON.** What is wrong with you?

**EDWARD.** Not a thing. Go on.

**ALLISON.** I haven't decided whether I prefer hard news or soft. Politics, sports, entertainment –

**EDWARD.** Talk about your tough choices.

**ALLISON.** All right! What is it?

**EDWARD.** Have I been unpleasant?

**ALLISON.** Yes!

**EDWARD.** My apologies. Maybe it's because my father died last month.

**ALLISON.** Why didn't you tell me?

**EDWARD.** Nothing you could do.

**ALLISON.** How's your mother?

**EDWARD.** Relieved.

(*short pause*)

Sorry. That was a rotten thing to say.

**ALLISON.** Was he sick a long time?

**EDWARD.** He had a stroke. He didn't hang on. In that sense he was lucky. I guess we all were.

**ALLISON.** You sound so callous.

**EDWARD.** He and I stopped talking years ago. This made it official.

**ALLISON.** That's all you have to say?

**EDWARD.** You met him.

**ALLISON.** Once.

**EDWARD.** That should've been sufficient.

**ALLISON.** He did a lot for you.

**EDWARD.** He paid the bills. He would've done the same thing for anyone who lived there.

**ALLISON.** Still, what's important is that –

**EDWARD.** What's important is that every time he walked into a room, I wanted to walk out! I hated the tension he brought with him, and a long time ago I made up my mind that I'd never live like that again. Whenever I think of him, I feel cold all over. I always did. I always will.

**ALLISON.** Should we talk about something else?

**EDWARD.** Please.

**ALLISON.** How's the job?

**EDWARD.** I edit every college publication.

**ALLISON.** Happy?

**EDWARD.** I keep busy.

**ALLISON.** Are you happy?

**EDWARD.** I think so. Even though I keep coming across these girls.

**ALLISON.** What girls?

**EDWARD.** Students. They all talk a mile a minute and bounce from one place to another. And they all have wonderful smiles. But no matter what they look like, they all remind me of someone else.

**ALLISON.** Met anybody interesting?

**EDWARD.** You mean women?

**ALLISON.** No, orangutans.

**EDWARD.** A few.

**ALLISON.** Details?

**EDWARD.** One French instructor.

**ALLISON.** *(with a French accent)* And what did you two talk about?

**EDWARD.** Her years in France.

**ALLISON.** I was there, too, you know.

**EDWARD.** She actually studied.

**ALLISON.** Have you met her family?

**EDWARD.** No.

**ALLISON.** What city are they from?

**EDWARD.** I don't know.

**ALLISON.** Do you know her name?

**EDWARD.** It's nothing serious.

*(short pause)*

**ALLISON.** I have to get to that shoot –

**EDWARD.** Anything else you want to tell me?

**ALLISON.** About what?

**EDWARD.** About that guy who works for the Mayor.

**ALLISON.** Oh, him! Well, he has a cosmopolitan charm.

**EDWARD.** He's slick.

**ALLISON.** I prefer smooth.

**EDWARD.** How about oily? Greasy? Oleaginous?

**ALLISON.** What about Joan of Arc?

**EDWARD.** A very scholarly woman.

**ALLISON.** Drippy.

**EDWARD.** Thoughtful.

**ALLISON.** Repressed.

**EDWARD.** Not at the motel.

**ALLISON.** You didn't.

**EDWARD.** How do you know?

**ALLISON.** I know.

(short pause)

I really want to do more on-camera.

**EDWARD.** You can do that anywhere.

**ALLISON.** Meaning what?

**EDWARD.** Meaning we have television around my place, too.

**ALLISON.** Are you inviting me to move there?

**EDWARD.** We have news shows.

**ALLISON.** In the woods? I can't interview a moose.

**EDWARD.** It's a beautiful town. Peaceful –

**ALLISON.** I'm not moving.

**EDWARD.** I didn't expect you to.

**ALLISON.** Then why'd you ask?

**EDWARD.** I was thinking out loud.

**ALLISON.** If we're going to talk about sacrifices...

**EDWARD.** Do you expect something from me?

**ALLISON.** I didn't say that.

**EDWARD.** Am I supposed to give up everything I've worked for?

**ALLISON.** Am I?

**EDWARD.** I think you have to make a choice.

**ALLISON.** About what?

**EDWARD.** About what matters to you most.

**ALLISON.** What about you? Don't you have to choose?

**EDWARD.** I've made a choice.

**ALLISON.** Oh, I can't wait to hear this.

**EDWARD.** I want what's best for both of us.

**ALLISON.** And, of course, you know what's best. For both of us.

**EDWARD.** I'm not sure, but –

**ALLISON.** Fine. While you work it out, I have a job to do.

**EDWARD.** *(to the audience)* During the next few years I received phone calls from all over the country.

**ALLISON.** Hello from Phoenix!

**EDWARD.** How'd you end up there?

**ALLISON.** I'm covering spring training. This morning I interviewed one of the White Sox. First I sat on his lap. Then he sat on mine.

**EDWARD.** Wonderful restaurants up here.

**ALLISON.** They had a magician on the morning show. He sawed me in half.

**EDWARD.** I'm trying my hand at writing science fiction.

**ALLISON.** I don't know which way to go. Some of the guys love to ferret through the garbage of some crooked judge, then expose him for stealing thirty-two dollars worth of pencils.

**EDWARD.** But all I get are rejections.

**ALLISON.** Some of the women do nothing but female stuff. Spousal abuse. Diseases. I don't want that, either. The world's depressing enough.

**EDWARD.** What do you want?

**ALLISON.** When I find it, I'll know.

*(to the audience)* Every year he sent me a birthday card. And every once in a while, completely out of the blue, another present.

**EDWARD.** *(to the audience)* I couldn't resist.

*(to her)*

How about a family?

**ALLISON.** Is that an offer?

**EDWARD.** I meant for you.

**ALLISON.** I'd better find the right guy first.

**EDWARD.** Anyone in mind?

**ALLISON.** A few possibilities.

**EDWARD.** You need only one. In fact, in most places, that's the legal limit.

**ALLISON.** I don't want to bore you.

**EDWARD.** Impossible.

**ALLISON.** For a while I dated Ronald.

**EDWARD.** Sounds like a high-tech kinda guy.

**ALLISON.** He's a model. Never caught him without his hair-dryer.

**EDWARD.** Enough said.

**ALLISON.** Then there was Arthur.

**EDWARD.** Definitely a high-tech guy.

**ALLISON.** Advertising executive. Very wealthy. Very appreciative of my talents. Unfortunately he felt the same way about several other women. Including his wife. Then I met Marco.

**EDWARD.** Now here's the high-tech guy!

**ALLISON.** Owns three trendy shoestores. Used to bring me all the latest styles. Loved to watch me try them on. Then take then off. Then try them on…

**EDWARD.** I get the picture.

**ALLISON.** What about you?

**EDWARD.** Several.

**ALLISON.** Several!

**EDWARD.** Now and then. Here and there.

**ALLISON.** Anybody I know?

**EDWARD.** I doubt it.

**ALLISON.** Anybody I should know?

**EDWARD.** I doubt it. Although there was one interesting girl. A kindergarten teacher. Very friendly.

**ALLISON.** But…?

**EDWARD.** Her furniture was so small. Tiny tables and chairs.

**ALLISON.** I get it.

**EDWARD.** And she kept trying to feed me graham crackers and grape juice.

**ALLISON.** Fine.

**EDWARD.** We did have some fun. Fingerpainting.

**ALLISON.** In other words, just a fling.

**EDWARD.** Nothing serious.

**ALLISON.** I'm sending you something.

**EDWARD.** A present?

**ALLISON.** Draft of an article I wrote. Fix it, and give it to me in Boston next week.

**EDWARD.** What's in Boston?

**ALLISON.** Monday night at seven.

**EDWARD.** Why?

**ALLISON.** Is there a problem?

**EDWARD.** No, but I was wondering –

**ALLISON.** Then be there. You have a suit?

**EDWARD.** Two.

**ALLISON.** Wear one.

**EDWARD.** Why?

**ALLISON.** Just do it.

**EDWARD.** But where are we going –

**ALLISON.** Just do it! Please.

**EDWARD.** *(to the audience)* I heard that voice, and I thought about those eyes. Even if I had wanted to, I couldn't have said no.

   *(They hug.)*

You haven't gained an ounce.

**ALLISON.** I battle my weight every day. The camera adds five pounds.

**EDWARD.** I thought it was ten.

**ALLISON.** Thanks so much.

   *(short pause)*

**EDWARD.** Your face is…radiant.

**ALLISON.** I know.

**EDWARD.** You're welcome. Why am I here?

**ALLISON.** I'm going to say this once, so don't interrupt. Tonight we're going to a party.

**EDWARD.** I don't understand –

**ALLISON.** You're interrupting. It's my high school reunion.

**EDWARD.** Congratulations. Why do you need me –

**ALLISON.** I know I'm being ridiculous, but I don't want to walk in alone. I know I should be able to, but I can't. I want to walk in with a man. So you're coming with me.

**EDWARD.** Fine.

**ALLISON.** Fine?

**EDWARD.** Do you have any idea how proud I'll be to stroll in with you?

**ALLISON.** Just do it.

**EDWARD.** *(to the audience)* It was less painful than I expected. Maybe because like the rest of the spouses and significant others, I was invisible. Except for one intriguing sequence, when she pointed me out to a friend.

**ALLISON.** "He's all mine."

**EDWARD.** *(to the audience)* I played along. When the friend asked if we were getting married, I said, "We've talked about it."

**ALLISON.** *(to the audience)* Then I said, "It's tough when our jobs are so far apart."

**EDWARD.** *(to the audience)* "But you never can tell. After all, she's the most alluring woman I have ever met."

**ALLISON.** *(to the audience)* I couldn't tell whether he was serious.

**EDWARD.** *(to the audience)* Neither could I. But I kept going. "Besides, I care more about her than I do about myself."

*(long pause)*

Back in her room, we were still confused.

*(They sit. She puts her feet in his lap, and he takes off her shoes. He drops one in front, and tosses the other aside.)*

**ALLISON.** Were you serious tonight?

**EDWARD.** When?

**ALLISON.** You know exactly when. Were you serious?

**EDWARD.** I don't know. Was I?

**ALLISON.** I asked you first.

**EDWARD.** Have you thought about it?

**ALLISON.** Marriage?

**EDWARD.** Of course.

**ALLISON.** Of course.

**EDWARD.** I mean to me.

**ALLISON.** The answer's still yes. How about you?

**EDWARD.** I've raised the question…hypothetically.

**ALLISON.** Me, too. I just wish I weren't on the road so much…

**EDWARD.** And my load at school…it never ends.

*(She sits up and puts her feet on the floor.)*

**ALLISON.** I just decided. Tonight was all an act.

**EDWARD.** For whom?

**ALLISON.** For you.

**EDWARD.** Did I say that?

**ALLISON.** I heard what you said. The question is, did you mean it?

**EDWARD.** Why is all this my responsibility?

**ALLISON.** I deserve an answer.

**EDWARD.** I was ordered to come here!

**ALLISON.** Are you sorry you did?

**EDWARD.** I didn't say that –

**ALLISON.** And I didn't order you to do anything!

**EDWARD.** Am I supposed to feel guilty?

**ALLISON.** Am I?

**EDWARD.** Then what am I doing here?

*(She walks away.)*

Having another drink?

**ALLISON.** Is there a problem?

**EDWARD.** You tell me. That's at least your sixth.

**ALLISON.** I haven't been counting.

**EDWARD.** I haven't, either, but it seems to me –

**ALLISON.** I'm fine.

**EDWARD.** I never said you weren't. I just –

**ALLISON.** I won't barf all over the room!

**EDWARD.** I'm glad!

**ALLISON.** I'm fine!

**EDWARD.** I'm happy for you!

**ALLISON.** I just didn't want to walk in alone!

**EDWARD.** Why not?

**ALLISON.** These people have lives. Families.

**EDWARD.** But a lot of them probably envy you.

**ALLISON.** So what?. Every day somebody tells me that the camera adores me. I am also told that I am perky. I exude perkiness. How would you like to be called "perky?"

**EDWARD.** I wouldn't look forward to it.

**ALLISON.** I hate "perky." I also hate "spunky" and "bouncy." They sound like three of Snow White's illegitimate dwarfs.

**EDWARD.** Are you getting better assignments?

**ALLISON.** I am the princess of fluff. My last scoop was ten ways to pack a suitcase.

**EDWARD.** Socks go in shoes, right?

**ALLISON.** That was number seven. Nine to go.

**EDWARD.** Should I send three dollars and a stamped envelope to – ?

**ALLISON.** Don't bother. In all these years, I've had one serious interview. A mother who lost her four-year-old son in a fire. I had to shove a microphone in her face and ask her how she felt. She broke down in front of me. I cried for a week.

**EDWARD.** I've never understood how people can deal with such terrible things.

**ALLISON.** There's one opening. Entertainment reporter.

**EDWARD.** Gossip.

**ALLISON.** Do you have to put it so crudely?

*(short pause)*

You ever lonely?

**EDWARD.** I keep busy. And I meet new people.

**ALLISON.** Sounds like you've forgotten all about me.

**EDWARD.** What is your name?

*(He smiles. She does not.)*

I meant to tell you. I liked your article.

**ALLISON.** About time you said so.

**EDWARD.** How you manage to make selling pigs at a county fair so entertaining is beyond me.

**ALLISON.** It wasn't easy. Anything need fixing?

**EDWARD.** Quite a bit, actually. The writing isn't as crisp as it should be. But that's understandable. You're out of practice.

**ALLISON.** Is that a shot at my job?

**EDWARD.** No. I'm just aware that you're concentrating in other areas.

**ALLISON.** Which in your opinion aren't worthwhile.

**EDWARD.** My only opinion is that you should keep writing.

**ALLISON.** I think about it.

**EDWARD.** Thinking doesn't help. You have to do it.

**ALLISON.** Don't push me.

**EDWARD.** I'm not pushing. But don't forget. You have real talent –

**ALLISON.** I can't stand being pushed!

**EDWARD.** It's just that it would be a shame for you to –

**ALLISON.** HEY! ENOUGH!

*(short pause)*

**EDWARD.** I hate to see ability wasted.

**ALLISON.** I'm not wasting anything!

**EDWARD.** I believe you!

**ALLISON.** Then what's your point?

**EDWARD.** Only that I want to see you do all you can.

**ALLISON.** I'm doing just fine!

**EDWARD.** I'm sure you are, but –

**ALLISON.** Don't patronize me!

**EDWARD.** I'm not! I'm just trying to say that I hope you'll –

**ALLISON.** AND WHO ARE YOU TO SAY ANYTHING TO ME?

*(pause)*

**EDWARD.** No one in particular.

**ALLISON.** I get up each day. I go to work. I come home. I take a plane. I take a cab. I take another plane. I talk to all these people. But no one...

**EDWARD.** Maybe the new job'll give you a chance to settle down.

**ALLISON.** I don't want to settle down!

**EDWARD.** I thought you said that –

**ALLISON.** I want to keep traveling!

**EDWARD.** Why?

**ALLISON.** I DON'T KNOW!

*(short pause)*

**EDWARD.** What do you want?

**ALLISON.** What do *you* want?

**EDWARD.** Basically what I have.

**ALLISON.** You're lying. Take off your clothes.

**EDWARD.** I beg your pardon.

**ALLISON.** Get 'em off!

**EDWARD.** You do it.

*(to the audience)* Within seconds she attacked.

**ALLISON.** *(to the audience)* We hit the bed.

**EDWARD.** *(to the audience)* The headboard nearly collapsed.

**ALLISON.** *(to the audience)* Then we moved to the floor. And knocked over the phone.

**EDWARD.** *(to the audience)* And a lamp.

**ALLISON.** *(to the audience)* I broke four nails on his back.

**EDWARD.** *(to the audience)* I almost dislocated my shoulder.

**ALLISON.** *(to the audience)* Then, for old times' sake...

**EDWARD.** *(to the audience)* We moved to the bathtub. It was too small.

**ALLISON.** *(to the audience)* It was perfect.

**EDWARD.** *(to the audience)* When I woke up the next morning, she was dressed.

**ALLISON.** *(holding one shoe)* Where's my other shoe?

*(He points. She picks up the shoe and walks away, carrying her shoes.)*

**EDWARD.** *(to the audience)* Over the next several years, things happened fast.

*(She puts on her shoes.)*

**ALLISON.** *(to the audience)* I got that job doing entertainment news.

**EDWARD.** *(to the audience)* I sent some fiction to an alum who ran a literary agency.

**ALLISON.** *(to the audience)* I kept traveling. New York to LA to France to England to New York to LA –

**EDWARD.** *(to the audience)* He didn't like it. But he had seen some material I put out for the school, and asked whether I'd edit a client's manuscript.

**ALLISON.** *(to the audience)* I lived in hotels.

**EDWARD.** *(to the audience)* At first I was reluctant. I wasn't ready to drop my own creative instincts.

**ALLISON.** *(to the audience)* Then I hit my big break. A spot on a national news magazine.

**EDWARD.** *(to the audience)* But deep down I knew I lacked Allison's abilities.

**ALLISON.** *(to the audience)* I moved to New York.

**EDWARD.** *(to the audience)* I also lacked Allison.

**ALLISON.** *(to the audience)* My first network position.

**EDWARD.** *(to the audience)* So I took on the project. It needed a total rewrite. But the agent was happy, the author was happy, and I had a new career.

**ALLISON.** *(to the audience)* The work was easy.

**EDWARD.** *(to the audience)* I did a couple of quickie bios, some pop psychology things, and a diet book. Amazing how many best-selling authors have no idea how to write.

**ALLISON.** *(to the audience)* "Guess what big-budget movie's in trouble?"

**EDWARD.** *(to the audience)* I worked ten hours a day. Weekends, too.

**ALLISON.** *(to the audience)* "And what party-loving TV hunk wrapped his car around a tree?"

**EDWARD.** *(to the audience)* I needed a jolt.

**ALLISON.** *(to the audience)* "The studio's keeping it hush-hush."

**EDWARD.** *(to the audience)* Guess who gave it to me.

**ALLISON.** *(to the audience)* "But we've found pictures."

**EDWARD.** *(to the audience)* By now she was almost famous.

**ALLISON.** *(to the audience)* Not that he ever called to congratulate me.

**EDWARD.** *(to the audience)* We met in Boston again. Eleven-thirty in the morning. I figured we'd have an early lunch.

*(She kisses him hard and long.)*

**ALLISON.** And how are you?

**EDWARD.** Busy. Doing all sorts of –

**ALLISON.** That's absolutely gripping. How's every little thing in the cloistered corridors of academia?

**EDWARD.** *(to the audience)* She wasn't exactly drunk, but she was way off.

*(to her)*

I'm more involved elsewhere.

**ALLISON.** Don't spare a single detail.

*(pause)*

**EDWARD.** You okay?

**ALLISON.** Did you see what I did? I asked a question, then waited for an answer. You hesitated, but I was shrewd enough to wait longer. That's the technique of a polished interviewer.

**EDWARD.** Wow.

**ALLISON.** That's why I'm a star. I am a star, you know.

**EDWARD.** I've seen you. You're a delight.

**ALLISON.** I tell about celebrities. The legendary personalities who shape our world and our dreams.

*(short pause)*

I know secrets. Wanna know a secret?

**EDWARD.** If you want to tell me.

**ALLISON.** Here's my secret: I'm sick of it all! Where's this school of yours?

**EDWARD.** Same place it's always been.

**ALLISON.** I want to go there. Now.

**EDWARD.** Why?

**ALLISON.** I want to see where you live. The people you know.

**EDWARD.** Why?

**ALLISON.** Start driving.

**EDWARD.** It's an hour and a half away.

**ALLISON.** Just do it!

**EDWARD.** *(to the audience)* I knew I was taking a chance, but even in this condition she was captivating.

**ALLISON.** Can't you drive faster?

*(short pause)*

Out where I am…you know, the world?

**EDWARD.** I've heard of it.

**ALLISON.** Everyone else covers crime, murder, war. Are you aware of any of this?

**EDWARD.** I try not to think about it.

**ALLISON.** The other night the show finished a three-part series on the homeless. They're living in boxes. Eating garbage.

*(short pause)*

I just finished a feature on the governor's mansion. Showcasing the new drapes.

*(short pause)*

One of the anchors is in love with me. Says he'll marry me as soon as he divorces his wife. And gets custody of his children.

*(short pause)*

**ALLISON.** *(cont.)* Over the past six months I've lost five assignments to the same woman. She's sleeping with the producer.

**EDWARD.** Ever think of moving?

**ALLISON.** Trying to get rid of me already?

**EDWARD.** No, I just meant that –

**ALLISON.** Besides, my mother's in bad shape.

**EDWARD.** I'm sorry.

**ALLISON.** And my father's not strong enough to take care of her. How can I leave?

*(short pause)*

Last week I found out that two of my best friends have cancer. One's terminal. She's forty-four years old. Husband and family. After she told me, I had to cover the dog show.

*(short pause)*

I don't want kids yet. I think I want 'em one day. Or *a* kid. They get sick a lot, don't they?

*(short pause)*

Every day people tell me that I make their lives happier. I also get lots of letters. Particularly from men who want to enrich my existence. And they offer the strangest suggestions how.

**EDWARD.** *(to the audience)* I didn't know what was coming out next, so I was glad when we turned into the campus and passed some students.

**ALLISON.** Isn't this cute.

**EDWARD.** It's comfy.

**ALLISON.** Think these kids have any idea what misery's waiting outside?

*(short pause)*

You're never leaving here, are you?

**EDWARD.** I don't know –

ALLISON. It's safe, and it's dull, and that's all you need, right?

EDWARD. *(to the audience)* That was the wrong moment to walk into the faculty club.

ALLISON. Is she here?

EDWARD. Who?

ALLISON. Your latest squeeze! From Sociology, right?

EDWARD. *(to the audience)* I would have given anything to escape, but unfortunately the lady in question waved to me.

*(to her)*

Over there.

Right in the middle of everyone.

ALLISON. She's charming! What's that thing around her shoulders? A horse blanket?

EDWARD. *(to the audience)* Much too loud. And suddenly...

ALLISON. It's a delight to meet you.

*(short pause)*

Oh, he and I are old friends! We go way back!

EDWARD. *(to the audience)* That's when I should've pulled her away, but I couldn't wait to hear what she'd say next.

ALLISON. No, I don't teach. I'm in television news.

*(short pause)*

Is that so? Well, maybe one day you'll buy a set. Then you'll know who I am.

EDWARD. *(to the audience)* That was enough.

*(He takes ALLISON's arm.)*

We have to go.

ALLISON. Tell me, how are you two doin'? Has he taken you to the bathtub?

EDWARD. Excuse me –

*(She shakes him off and speaks even louder.)*

**ALLISON.** He'll give you a real good scrubbin'!

**EDWARD.** We should press on –

**ALLISON.** Have you had sex with him yet?

**EDWARD.** *(to the audience)* She was practically shouting now. Every eye in the place was on us.

**ALLISON.** What are you waiting for? Where else are you going to find a man who's so open and caring?

**EDWARD.** Pardon us!

*(He tries to pull her away, but she fights him off.)*

**ALLISON.** Hasn't he asked? Then I guess it's nothing serious!

**EDWARD.** I'm sorry!

**ALLISON.** What about the rest of you ladies? Has he slept with any of you?

*(He tries to pull her away, but she fights him off.)*

**EDWARD.** She's had a couple of drinks!

**ALLISON.** It won't mean anything! You'll hit the sheets, and the next day he'll hardly know who you are!

**EDWARD.** All right –

**ALLISON.** Oh, you'll get the occasional phone call!

**EDWARD.** Let's get out of here!

**ALLISON.** He'll tell you all about his job! Ever notice how much fun he has when you're not around?

*(*EDWARD *manages to pull her away.)*

The man's a DAMNED ICICLE!

*(He sits her down. Long pause.)*

Aren't you going to introduce me to any more of your friends?

*(long pause)*

**EDWARD.** *(to the audience)* I was planning to leave the school anyway.

**ALLISON.** *(to the audience)* The whole time I was yelling I knew exactly what I was doing. But I couldn't stop myself.

**EDWARD.** *(to the audience)* On the way out, she walked ahead of me. Wouldn't even look me in the eye.

*(to her)*

You want a ride back to Boston?

**ALLISON.** Is there a bus?

**EDWARD.** Hm-mm.

**ALLISON.** I'll take the bus.

**EDWARD.** *(to the audience)* So I drove her to the terminal. Neither of us talked. I knew that inside we were both churning, and that I ought to do something, but I wasn't sure what, and I certainly didn't want to blurt out the wrong thing. After all, one misplaced word, and...

**ALLISON.** You don't have to wait.

**EDWARD.** I know.

**ALLISON.** I said you don't have to wait.

**EDWARD.** I know.

**ALLISON.** That's a polite way of telling you to get the hell away.

**EDWARD.** I know.

**ALLISON.** Are you going to yell at me?

**EDWARD.** No.

**ALLISON.** You expect an apology?

*(to the audience)* For the next few minutes, we stood silently, just staring ahead. Two women asked for my autograph. I think they wondered what I was doing at a bus terminal. So did I.

**EDWARD.** *(to the audience)* Finally the bus was ready to leave.

**ALLISON.** Well.

**EDWARD.** Well.

*(She holds out her hand. He kisses her.)*

Goodbye.

**ALLISON.** *(to the audience)* Was he really saying goodbye? Or was he forgiving me? I had no idea.

**EDWARD.** *(to the audience)* I didn't, either. I should have been furious. I mean, I worked with those people! But I understood what she was going through, so I couldn't be angry. The whole day was embarrassing. No, it was humiliating. But as I drove back, one thought kept recurring: that day was the most interesting one I'd ever spent at the college.

**ALLISON.** *(to the audience)* I was frustrated at everybody and everything, and I had to let it out.

**EDWARD.** *(to the audience)* Although that icicle crack...that stung. But it did have an element of truth.

**ALLISON.** *(to the audience)* I calmed down at work.

**EDWARD.** *(to the audience)* I left the college. I had more outside assignments than I could handle, and they were more fun than rewriting the catalogue.

**ALLISON.** *(to the audience)* The show hired a new producer. A woman. I traveled to Tokyo. South America. I wondered how he was, but I didn't always have a chance to...

**EDWARD.** *(to the audience)* I moved to the Northeast corner of Connecticut. I didn't call, but she was never out of my mind.

**ALLISON.** *(to the audience)* I didn't hear from him for a long time. Until I received a card at the station. "Happy Birthday. As ever, E." He included his address. But no telephone number.

**EDWARD.** *(to the audience)* If she wanted to call me, she'd have to look it up.

**ALLISON.** *(to the audience)* I didn't have a chance. My doctor found a small lump, and I went into the hospital for a biopsy. I never let him know, so I never expected him to show up. But the first afternoon, that face came poking around the door.

*(to him)*

How did you get here?

**EDWARD.** Car.

**ALLISON.** That's not what I mean.

**EDWARD.** I know.

*(He looks around, uncomfortable.)*

**ALLISON.** Are you all right?

**EDWARD.** Did I ever mention that I hate hospitals?

**ALLISON.** Frequently.

**EDWARD.** I hate the smell, and I hate the scrubs. I also hate long trips. And you know I'm not crazy about New York. But…

**ALLISON.** You love me.

*(short pause)*

**EDWARD.** Why didn't you tell me about this?

**ALLISON.** I didn't want to worry you.

**EDWARD.** Who else do I have to worry about? How are you feeling?

**ALLISON.** Sleepy.

**EDWARD.** I won't stay long.

**ALLISON.** It's all right. I'm glad you're here.

**EDWARD.** So…do they know anything yet?

**ALLISON.** Tomorrow.

**EDWARD.** You must be a wreck.

**ALLISON.** I've had better days.

**EDWARD.** So have I. Do you need anything? Something I can get?

**ALLISON.** Not a thing.

**EDWARD.** You're sure?

**ALLISON.** I'm sure.

**EDWARD.** Okay. But if you do think of something, I'll be at this number.

**ALLISON.** You're staying over? In the city?

**EDWARD.** I can't go back until I know what's going on. I mean, I can't work. I can't…

*(pause)*

**ALLISON.** You should've called. I look terrible.

**EDWARD.** I've seen you a lot worse.

**ALLISON.** Thank you so much.

**EDWARD.** But I'm in love with you, so what do I know?

**ALLISON.** *(to the audience)* He had never used the word before. Then he sat next to my bed and held my hand.

**EDWARD.** *(to the audience)* I babbled a bit. I don't remember what I said.

**ALLISON.** *(to the audience)* I hardly listened. I was just so happy to have him there.

**EDWARD.** *(to the audience)* Eventually a nurse told me to leave.

**ALLISON.** *(to the audience)* That's when he took out a small box, opened it, and pulled out a pendant. He slipped it around my neck, smiled, kissed me, and said he'd be back early the next day. I cried for…oh, only a few hours.

**EDWARD.** *(to the audience)* The thought of losing her was almost more than I could handle. I didn't find the right words, but I think she knew how I felt.

**ALLISON.** *(to the audience)* He managed to keep his composure, but he was shaken.

**EDWARD.** *(to the audience)* That night, I slept about twenty minutes. First thing the next morning, I was at the hospital.

*(pause)*

**ALLISON.** The results were negative.

**EDWARD.** That's what we wanted to hear, right?

**ALLISON.** Right.

**EDWARD.** So you're fine.

**ALLISON.** Hm-mm. I'll rest today, then go home tomorrow.

**EDWARD.** All better?

**ALLISON.** All better.

**EDWARD.** They're sure about it?

**ALLISON.** Yup.

**EDWARD.** You're absolutely okay.

**ALLISON.** Absolutely.

*(to the audience)* He must have asked six times.

**EDWARD.** *(to the audience)* I couldn't help it.

**ALLISON.** I'm glad you came.

**EDWARD.** Well, I have an interest here, too. After all, what would happen to me if you weren't around?

**ALLISON.** You wouldn't have anyone to clean up after.

**EDWARD.** No one would give me any problems.

**ALLISON.** And I couldn't leave you that way.

**EDWARD.** I should say not.

**ALLISON.** *(to the audience)* Soon after I left the hospital, I was back on the road.

**EDWARD.** *(to the audience)* I kept up by watching the show. When I couldn't see her, I'd sit on my porch and dream about her.

**ALLISON.** *(to the audience)* Then one night, in the middle of all the craziness, I met Jerry.

**EDWARD.** *(to the audience)* I never figured she'd meet someone serious.

**ALLISON.** *(to the audience)* He was successful, good-looking, and nuts about me. Nothing new there. But he surprised me by getting down to business so soon. I must have been in a receptive mood, because before I knew what was happening, I found myself engaged.

**EDWARD.** *(to the audience)* Then, out of the blue, she called. Her book was one reason. Yet I couldn't help feeling she had something else on her mind. That's why I didn't jump when she asked me to do it.

**ALLISON.** *(to the audience)* Was I giving him one last chance?

**EDWARD.** *(to the audience)* She showed up at three-thirty. Early enough so she could drive home that night, late enough so that if she dilly-dallied…oh, I explained that already.

**ALLISON.** I'm hungry.

**EDWARD.** Coachman's waiting. Flounder and bluefish broiling even as we speak.

**ALLISON.** Will I get back in time to drive home?

**EDWARD.** If that's what you want.

**ALLISON.** Is that what you want?

**EDWARD.** What about…what's his name?

**ALLISON.** Joey.

**EDWARD.** Jerry!

**ALLISON.** *(to the audience)* We headed off in his car.

**EDWARD.** *(to the audience)* Dinner went fine.

**ALLISON.** *(to the audience)* A little heavy on the Formica.

**EDWARD.** *(to the audience)* The waitress couldn't believe who was with me. Neither could I.

**ALLISON.** *(to the audience)* I usually gobbled my food in minutes. Tonight we dawdled for an hour over dessert and coffee.

*(to him)*

How do you spend your time?

**EDWARD.** Publishers send me manuscripts with problems. I solve the problems.

**ALLISON.** Why do they choose you?

**EDWARD.** Why?

**ALLISON.** I asked you first.

**EDWARD.** I'm the best.

**ALLISON.** And modest, too. Do you advertise?

**EDWARD.** I don't have to.

**ALLISON.** Does it pay?

**EDWARD.** I have everything I want. Except you.

*(short pause)*

**ALLISON.** Are you happy?

**EDWARD.** People send me their thoughts and emotions sprawled over hundreds of pages. I put everything in order.

**ALLISON.** Are you happy?

**EDWARD.** I have fewer worries than anyone I know.

**ALLISON.** But are you happy?

*(pause)*

**EDWARD.** All the married people I meet, especially the ones with children, they're always nervous. I'm calm.

Because everything I do stops with me. After I'm finished...

*(a beat)*

I'm finished. Sometimes, though, that's frightening.
Sometimes I think I've been by myself long enough.

*(short pause)*

How about this book they asked for? You want to write
it?

**ALLISON.** My publisher calls me one of the hot new faces.

**EDWARD.** What does your fiancé call you?

**ALLISON.** Babe.

**EDWARD.** That's kinda sweet. If you're a big blue ox or a fat
rightfielder.

*(to the audience)* Then we headed back to my house.

**ALLISON.** This place does have a peculiar charm.

**EDWARD.** There's a beautiful grove out back. I like it when
the sun goes down and a breeze blows in.

**ALLISON.** The other night Jerry's family had me over for
dinner. His mother told everybody how wonderful I
was, that if anyone could bring up children and take
care of a house and have a career and make Jerry the
happiest man in the world, it was me. I'm worn out
already.

*(short pause)*

Why am I writing a book? What do I have to say?

*(short pause)*

Do you ever wish you were back in college?

*(a beat)*

Can I stay here tonight?

**EDWARD.** *(to the audience)* Did she just want to run away
from everything else? Or...?

**ALLISON.** Did I ever tell you about the best story I ever did?
My favorite, anyway.

**EDWARD.** The circus. When you interviewed the clowns.

**ALLISON.** No.

**EDWARD.** The Brooklyn Bridge Anniversary?

**ALLISON.** The newspaper dealer.

**EDWARD.** I don't remember this one.

**ALLISON.** He had been at the same stand for forty years. In a building on 55th street. Just selling newspapers, candy, and lottery tickets. He was retiring, so they gave him a party, and we came to shoot it. He had been married for thirty-nine years, and he had a couple of kids. He told me that the newspaper stand and his family were his entire world. He also told me that he thought he was happier than any man he had ever known.

**EDWARD.** You should write about him.

**ALLISON.** He's not worth a whole book.

**EDWARD.** But he's worth a story. And you probably have dozens like him.

**ALLISON.** I'm not sure how to put it all together.

**EDWARD.** We can do it. Besides, those profiles have always been your best work. You have a real knack for bringing people to life.

**ALLISON.** I do?

**EDWARD.** Even the most unlikely ones.

*(short pause)*

**ALLISON.** You ever see anybody from school?

**EDWARD.** Just you.

**ALLISON.** I saw Emily Sherman. She's a lawyer for the IRS.

**EDWARD.** She was always a tiger. Remember her playing basketball?

**ALLISON.** I met Kevin Breger in a bookstore. He's a chef. Still thin as a rail. Brian's a urologist. Apparently very gifted.

**EDWARD.** I don't care to know the standards for evaluation.

**ALLISON.** They're all settled down.

**EDWARD.** *(to the audience)* I asked if she wanted to take a walk.

**ALLISON.** *(to the audience)* We went around the yard. Then through that grove.

**EDWARD.** *(to the audience)* She did most of the talking.

**ALLISON.** *(to the audience)* I told him stories he had heard before.

**EDWARD.** *(to the audience)* She needed to tell them.

**ALLISON.** *(to the audience)* He listened the way he always did. Then I talked about Jerry.

**EDWARD.** *(to the audience)* And Jerry's mother.

**ALLISON.** *(to the audience)* My mother.

**EDWARD.** *(to the audience)* Her father.

**ALLISON.** *(to the audience)* My boss. My friends.

**EDWARD.** *(to the audience)* College.

**ALLISON.** *(to the audience)* Children.

**EDWARD.** *(to the audience)* Children she knew. Children she imagined.

**ALLISON.** *(to the audience)* Remembering what it was like to be young.

**EDWARD.** *(to the audience)* Wondering what it'll be like to be old.

**ALLISON.** *(to the audience)* I put my arm through his.

**EDWARD.** *(to the audience)* She laid her head on my shoulder.

**ALLISON.** *(to the audience)* It belonged there.

**EDWARD.** *(to the audience)* We were back the way we were.

**ALLISON.** *(to the audience)* The way it had never been with anyone else.

**EDWARD.** *(to the audience)* The way it never could be with anyone else.

**ALLISON.** *(to the audience)* The air held a lovely late summer tang. Perfect.

**EDWARD.** *(to the audience)* I knew that if we could keep everything the way it was at that moment, I could be happy. I wanted time to stop. To make it all easy for me. But the planet kept spinning. And the light began to fade. When we came close to the house, we heard her cell phone ringing.

**ALLISON.** *(to the audience)* Jerry. I wasn't ready for him.

*(to the phone)*

Hi.

**EDWARD.** *(to the audience)* I could tell by the way she said it. He wasn't right for her.

**ALLISON.** Yes, I told him all about you. He said you had to be special.

**EDWARD.** *(to the audience)* If he needed all this encouragement, he obviously lacked pizzazz.

**ALLISON.** I'll be back tonight.

*(a beat)*

Right. Right. Okay. 'Bye.

**EDWARD.** *(to the audience)* By now I resented his calling. Didn't he know she was with me?

**ALLISON.** If I change my plans, I'll call you.

*(short pause)*

I said I'll call.

**EDWARD.** *(to the audience)* He was pushy, too. That's when it hit me: I finally knew what I had to do.

**ALLISON.** Right. 'Bye. Right. 'Bye.

*(to him)*

He wants to meet for a late supper.

**EDWARD.** You have room after all that flounder?

**ALLISON.** He gets hungry.

**EDWARD.** I understand.

*(short pause)*

Did I tell you I'm seeing the town librarian?

**ALLISON.** Really. I'm sure she's very quiet.

**EDWARD.** Demure.

**ALLISON.** Dull.

*(to the audience)* He wanted me to take over. I wanted to hear it from him.

**EDWARD.** *(to the audience)* I was getting there.

*(to her)*

How is he?

ALLISON. Fine.

EDWARD. He sounded kinda buffaloed.

ALLISON. He's perfectly capable.

EDWARD. He'd better be. Poor guy.

ALLISON. What's that supposed to mean?

EDWARD. How's he ever going to take care of you?

ALLISON. No one takes care of me! I run my own life –

EDWARD. Look at your car. Cans, cups, wrappers, news-papers...

ALLISON. What's your point?

EDWARD. Somebody's gotta clean this up.

ALLISON. Somebody will.

EDWARD. Not Jerry!

ALLISON. Maybe not, but –

EDWARD. He's a busy man! And what about your apart-ment? It's a disaster, isn't it?

ALLISON. You haven't even seen it.

EDWARD. Clothes everywhere! Shoes in the refrigerator! Food in the bathroom –

ALLISON. There are no shoes in the –

EDWARD. And your bankbook's nothing but scribbles, right!?

ALLISON. Why do you assume –

EDWARD. Am I right?

ALLISON. You could say that.

EDWARD. And Jerry's not going to have time for all this non-sense! He's got responsibilities! Importing, exporting! Exporting, importing! I also think you need another place to leave your stuff. All the overflow!

ALLISON. I can always ask Jerry to take –

EDWARD. Jerry, Joey, Jimmy! He's not in your league!

ALLISON. How do you know?

**EDWARD.** And even if he were, he's not prepared for all this! No one would be. Unless they know you. And all your little...quirks.

**ALLISON.** What quirks?

**EDWARD.** Let's face it. You need an extra-special fella. And...

**ALLISON.** And...?

**EDWARD.** And I'm the only one I know!

*(He turns away and steadies himself.)*

**ALLISON.** *(to the audience)* Was he going to stop there?

**EDWARD.** *(to the audience)* I couldn't come right out and ask.

**ALLISON.** *(to the audience)* Instead he dug his hand into his pocket and pulled out a key ring.

**EDWARD.** Front door and back door.

*(He places a key in her hand.)*

Any time you want. As long as you want.

*(to the audience)* Would she understand? I couldn't breathe.

*(pause)*

**ALLISON.** This woman you claim to be seeing.

**EDWARD.** What do you mean, "claim to be?" We've gone to dinner three times in the –

**ALLISON.** Exactly what does she do?

**EDWARD.** I told you. She works at the library.

**ALLISON.** Right, right. I assume she's easy-going.

**EDWARD.** Completely affable.

**ALLISON.** Never annoys you.

**EDWARD.** Utterly congenial.

**ALLISON.** Does she ever take you places you don't want to visit? Make you meet people you don't want to know?

**EDWARD.** No. In fact, it's just the opposite –

**ALLISON.** Does she ever interrupt you?

**EDWARD.** Absolutely not.

**ALLISON.** Try to run your life?

**EDWARD.** Not at all –

**ALLISON.** Then what use is she?

*(She walks away. He turns her around and kisses her passionately. When they break, he smiles.)*

**EDWARD.** Would you care to reconsider that icicle remark?

*(He smiles to the audience.)*

**ALLISON.** *(to the audience)* I didn't go back to New York until the next day.

**EDWARD.** *(to the audience)* By the time she left, the engagement to Jerry was off.

**ALLISON.** *(to the audience)* If it had ever really been on. Now all I had to do was tell Jerry.

**EDWARD.** *(to the audience)* I had nothing to contribute, so I kept quiet.

**ALLISON.** *(to the audience)* I didn't want to hurt the guy. After all, I did care for him. But compared to this one...

**EDWARD.** *(to the audience)* Thank you very much.

**ALLISON.** *(to the audience)* The minute I walked into Jerry's office, though, I realized that he knew.

**EDWARD.** *(to the audience)* When she told me about it, I almost felt sorry for him.

**ALLISON.** *(to the audience)* His mother took it just fine.

*(short pause)*

For the first time that I could remember, I felt... together.

*(short pause)*

My world didn't change overnight, of course. I still had people to see and places to go.

**EDWARD.** *(to the audience)* I wouldn't want it any other way. Besides, I love her stories. And who else is going to listen?

**ALLISON.** *(to the audience)* And I love telling them. But only to him.

**EDWARD.** *(to the audience)* She's finally realized that I'm the only one who can make her happy.

**ALLISON.** *(to the audience)* And he's finally figured out that I'm the only one he wants to make happy.

**EDWARD.** *(to the audience)* These days I visit New York regularly. Primarily for the pleasure of editing her book. And her life.

**ALLISON.** *(to the audience)* I've moved a lot of my stuff into his house. In fact, I've taken over two closets.

**EDWARD.** *(to the audience)* Let's face it. The whole room is hers. Although we regularly share it to our mutual satisfaction.

**ALLISON.** *(to the audience)* Big bathtub.

*(short pause)*

I try to keep things neat.

**EDWARD.** *(to the audience)* No, she doesn't. But I don't care! Last month she spent her vacation here. By the time she left, practically the whole town had visited for dinner.

**ALLISON.** *(to the audience)* Except the staff of the library.

**EDWARD.** *(to the audience)* Even some of her newsroom friends drove out to see us. My circle of acquaintances is widening at a terrifying rate.

**ALLISON.** *(to the audience)* I've eaten that corn at least a half a dozen times. Now I'm looking at trees. I never imagined that I could…

*(She looks at **EDWARD**, then the audience.)*

Yes, I did.

**EDWARD.** *(to the audience)* Oh. A final piece of news.

**ALLISON.** *(to the audience)* You must've guessed.

**EDWARD.** *(to the audience)* We're getting married. To each other.

**ALLISON.** *(to the audience)* The details have to be worked out, of course. Endless problems.

**EDWARD.** *(to the audience)* Why am I looking forward to all of them?

**ALLISON.** *(to the audience)* There's just something about him.

**EDWARD.** *(to the audience)* In fact, I've been thinking about the honeymoon.

**ALLISON.** *(to the audience)* I've got it all planned. We're going to the Grand Canyon. I missed it the last time I went out there. I can't wait to ride one of those burros all the way down to the bottom.

(**EDWARD** *looks at her, then turns to the audience.*)

**EDWARD.** *(to the audience)* As we said, some details have to be worked out. A few even more important than that.

**ALLISON.** For instance?

**EDWARD.** The house. Our finances.

**ALLISON.** I don't think those are necessarily more important –

**EDWARD.** Children.

**ALLISON.** Pardon me?

**EDWARD.** I thought you wanted them.

**ALLISON.** You always said you didn't.

**EDWARD.** I've changed my mind.

**ALLISON.** Why?

**EDWARD.** Because now I'll be having them with you. And the thought of a little Allison running around the house is irresistible.

**ALLISON.** She'll be charming, won't she?

**EDWARD.** She'll certainly tell everybody she is.

**ALLISON.** Of course, it might be a little Edward.

**EDWARD.** Could there be such a thing?

**ALLISON.** It's a scary thought. He'll probably vacuum his own nursery.

**EDWARD.** I love him already.

**ALLISON.** *(to the audience)* What's left to say? Just that life's a funny business.

**EDWARD.** *(to the audience)* One day you think you have everything mapped out.

**ALLISON.** *(to the audience)* Then something unexpected knocks you for a loop.

**EDWARD.** *(to the audience)* And while you're trying to figure out where you stand...

**ALLISON.** *(to the audience)* Something else happens. And you find yourself starting all over again.

*(She begins to pull him offstage, but he stops her and gently spins her back to him as if they are dancing. They end up with his arm around her. She kisses him, and puts her arm around him.)*

**EDWARD.** *(to the audience)* Of course, if you're lucky...

**ALLISON.** *(to the audience)* Very lucky...it all works out.

**EDWARD.** *(to the audience)* The way you always dreamed.

*(They smile at each other. He invites her offstage, and together they leave.)*

## CURTAIN

# Also by
## Victor L. Cahn...

# Fit to Kill

# Roses in December